In My Backyard

I SEE A CHIPMUNK

By Alex Appleby

Gareth Stevens
Publishing

Please visit our website, www.garethstevens.com. For a free color catalog of all our high-quality books, call toll free 1-800-542-2595 or fax 1-877-542-2596.

Library of Congress Cataloging-in-Publication Data

Appleby, Alex.
 I see a chipmunk / Alex Appleby.
    p. cm. — (In my backyard)
 Includes index.
 ISBN 978-1-4339-8548-5 (pbk.)
 ISBN 978-1-4339-8549-2 (6-pack)
 ISBN 978-1-4339-8547-8 (library binding)
 1. Chipmunks—Juvenile literature. I. Title.
 QL737.R68A66 2013
 599.36'4—dc23
                                        2012020691

First Edition

Published in 2013 by
Gareth Stevens Publishing
111 East 14th Street, Suite 349
New York, NY 10003

Copyright © 2013 Gareth Stevens Publishing

Editor: Ryan Nagelhout
Designer: Katelyn Londino

Photo credits: Cover, pp. 1, 5, 9, 15 iStockphoto/Thinkstock.com; p. 7 Kateryna Dyellalova/Shutterstock.com; pp. 11, 24 (acorn) Sarah Cates/Shutterstock.com; pp. 13, 24 (pouches) Tolmachevr/Shutterstock.com; p. 17 Margaret M Stewart/Shutterstock.com; p. 19 Leonard Lee Rue III/Photo Reasearchers/Getty Images; pp. 21, 24 (den) STEVE MASALOWSKI/Photo Researchers/Getty Images; p. 23 Bob Gurr/All Canada Photos/Getty Images.

Printed in the United States of America

CPSIA compliance information: Batch #CW13GS: For further information contact Gareth Stevens, New York, New York at 1-800-542-2595.

Contents

A chipmunk is
a small squirrel.
There are 25 kinds!

It loves to climb trees!

7

It eats nuts and seeds.

It gathers up to 165 acorns a day!

11

Its has pouches
in its cheeks. They get
filled with food!

13

It digs a hole to live in.
This is called its den.

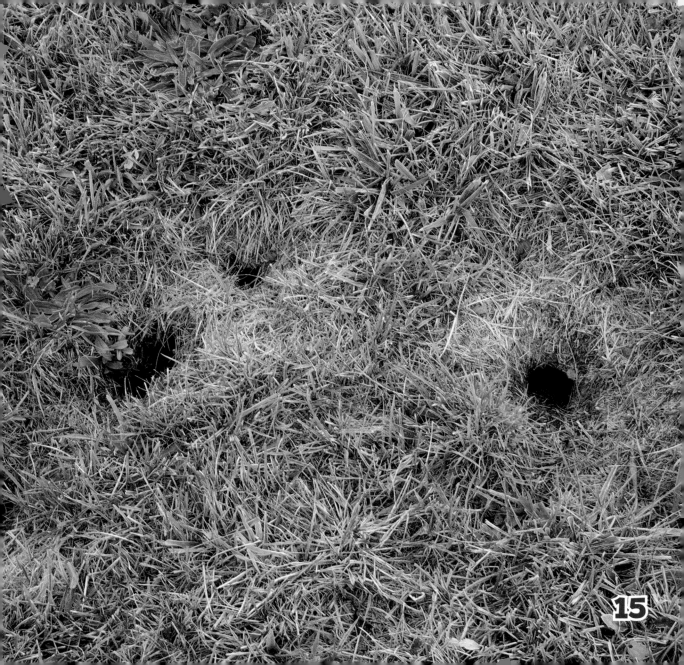

15

Its den has two rooms.

One is to sleep in.

19

The other is to hold
its food!

21

A chipmunk stays there in winter. This is called hibernation.

23

Words to Know

acorns

den

pouches

Index

24